THE DEVIL'S STORYBOOK

The Devil's Storybook

STORIES AND PICTURES

BY NATALIE BABBITT

FARRAR · STRAUS · GIROUX

NEW YORK

Copyright © 1974 by Natalie Babbitt
All rights reserved
Library of Congress catalog card number: 74–5488
Published in Canada by
McGraw-Hill Ryerson Ltd., Toronto
Printed in the United States of America
Designed by Cynthia Krupat
First edition, 1974
Fourth printing, 1978

CONTENTS

From his brimstone bed, at break of day,
    A-walking the Devil is gone,
To look at his little snug farm of the World,
    And see how his stock went on.

ROBERT SOUTHEY (1774-1843)

THE DEVIL'S STORYBOOK

WISHES

ONE DAY when things were dull in Hell, the Devil fished around in his bag of disguises, dressed himself as a fairy godmother, and came up into the World to find someone to bother. He wandered down the first country road he came to and before long he met a crabby farm wife stumping along with a load of switches on her back.

"Good morning, my dear," said the Devil in his best fairy-godmother voice. "It's a fine day, isn't it?"

"It's not," said the farm wife. "There hasn't been a fine day in the World in twenty years."

"That long?" said the Devil.

"That long," she snapped.

Now, it was the Devil's plan that morning to make a nuisance of himself by granting wishes, and he decided there was no time like now to begin. "See here then," he said to the farm wife. "I will grant you one wish—anything at all—and that ought to cheer you up."

"One wish?" said the farm wife.

"One," he replied.

"Very well," said the farm wife. "Here's my wish. Since I don't believe in fairy godmothers, I wish you'd go back where you came from and leave me alone."

This wish caught the Devil off guard and before he knew it he had landed with a bump in his throne room in Hell. Up he rose, his hair on end with anger. "That's one I'll get someday, anyway," he said to himself, and back he went to the World to find another victim.

The next soul he met was a very old man who sat under a tree staring away at nothing.

"Good morning, old man," said the Devil in his

best fairy-godmother voice. "It's a fine day, isn't it?"

"One of many," said the old man. "One of many."

The Devil didn't like this answer at all. It sounded too contented. "See here then," he said to the old man. "I will grant you one wish—anything at all—but I can guess what you'll choose to wish for."

"What's that?" said the old man.

"Why," said the Devil, "seeing as your life is nearly done, my guess is you'll wish to be a boy again."

The old man pulled at his whiskers for a while and then he said, "No, not that. It was good to be a boy, but not *all* good."

"Then," pursued the Devil, "you'll wish to return to young manhood."

"No," said the old man. "It was good to be a young man, but still—it was difficult, too. No, that wouldn't be my wish."

The Devil began to feel annoyed. "Well then," he said, "surely you'll wish to be once more in your prime, a hearty soul of forty or fifty."

"No," said the old man, "I wouldn't wish that. It was good to be forty and good to be fifty, but those times were often hard as well."

"What age will you wish to be, then?" barked the Devil, losing his patience at last.

"Why should I want to be any age but this one?" said the old man. "That was *your* idea. One time is as good as another, and just as bad, too, for that matter. I'd wish for something different—I don't know what —if I really had a wish."

"Well," said the Devil, "I've changed my mind anyway. You *don't* have a wish."

"I didn't think I did," said the old man, and he went back to staring away at nothing.

The Devil ground his teeth and smoke came out of his ears, but he went on down the road until at last he came to a vain young man in fancy clothes riding on a big brown horse. "Good morning, young man," said the Devil in his best fairy-godmother voice. "It's a fine day, isn't it?"

"Indeed it is, dear madam," said the vain young man, taking off his hat and bowing as well as he could from the saddle.

"Well now," said the Devil, "you're such a fine young man, I think I'll grant you a wish. One wish, anything you like. What do you say to that?"

"A wish?" cried the vain young man, dropping his hat. "Anything I want? Can it really be true?"

"It can," said the Devil, smiling. "What will you wish for?"

"Dear me!" said the vain young man. "Anything at all? I could wish to be rich, couldn't I!"

"You could," said the Devil.

"But on the other hand I could wish that all the girls would fall in love with me," said the vain young man, beginning to grow excited. "Or I could wish to be the Crown Prince. Or the King! I could even wish to rule the whole World, as far as that goes."

"You could," said the Devil, smiling more than ever.

"Or I could wish to stay young and handsome for-ever," said the vain young man.

"You could," said the Devil.

"But wait!" cried the vain young man. "Perhaps it would be better to wish for perfect health. What good are all those other things if you're too sick to enjoy them?"

"True," said the Devil.

"Oh, dear," moaned the vain young man, wringing his hands. "What to wish for! What to choose! I shall go quite mad, trying to decide! Health, power, money, love, endless youth, each a perfect wish all by itself. Sweet fairy godmother, I wish you'd *tell* me what to wish for!"

"If that's what you want, all right," said the Devil with a smile as big as the moon. "Most people think the best wish of all is to wish that every wish they ever wish will always come true."

The young man's eyes grew round and his cheeks paled. "Yes. Yes!" he said. "They're right, of course.

That *is* the best. All right, so here I go. I wish that every wish I ever wish will always come true."

"Too late," said the Devil gleefully.

The young man stared. "Too late?" he cried. "But why? You said I could wish for anything, didn't you?"

"I did," grinned the Devil. "That's true. But you used up your wish when you wished I'd tell you what to wish for!"

And with the young man's wail of chagrin ringing in his ears, the Devil went back down to Hell, well satisfied at last.

THE VERY PRETTY
LADY

THERE WAS a very pretty lady once who lived all alone. She didn't have to live all alone; she was so pretty that there were many young men anxious to marry her. They hung about in her dooryard and played guitars and sang sweet songs and tried to look in through the windows. They were there from dawn to dusk, always sad, always hopeful. But the very pretty lady didn't want to marry any of them. "It's no use being loved for the way one looks," she said to herself. "If I can't find someone who will love me in spite of my face, then I will never marry anyone at all."

This was wise, no doubt, but no one is wise all the

time. For the truth is that the very pretty lady rather liked the fact that she was pretty, and sometimes she would stand in front of the mirror and look and look at herself. At times like that she would be pleased with herself and would go out to the dooryard and talk to all the young men and let them go with her to market and carry home her bags and packages for her. And for a long time afterward they would all look a good deal more hopeful than sad.

But most of the time the very pretty lady stayed inside her cottage, feeling lonely regardless of all the young men in the dooryard, longing for someone who would love her as she wanted to be loved.

Now, after a while, one way or another, the Devil heard about the very pretty lady and he decided that she was the very thing he needed to brighten up his days in Hell. So he packed a satchel of disguises and went up to have a look at her.

He had heard how very pretty she was, but no one had told him that she never let anyone inside the cottage. He went disguised as a beggar, but she wouldn't open the door. He tried appearing as a preacher and then as a king, but that didn't work either. So at last he simply disguised himself as one of her suitors and hung about with the others waiting for market day.

When the pretty lady came out at last, the Devil walked beside her all the way to town, looking at her every moment, and he carried back the heaviest package. By the time she had gone inside her cottage again, his mind was made up: she was indeed exactly what he needed in Hell, and he had waited long enough to have her.

When night came and the sad and hopeful young men had all gone home, the Devil threw off his disguise and wished himself into the pretty lady's bedroom with a puff of red smoke and a noise like thunder. The pretty lady woke up at once, and when she saw him she shrieked.

"Don't be alarmed," said the Devil calmly. "It's only me. I've come to take you away to Hell."

"Never!" cried the pretty lady. "I shan't go and there's no way you can make me."

"That's true," said the Devil, "there isn't. You have to come of your own free will when you come before your time. But you'll like it so much down there—you'll be the prettiest thing in the place."

"I'm that already, right here," said the pretty lady, "for all the good it does me. Why should I go away to have the same thing somewhere else?"

"Ah, but in Hell," said the Devil, "your beauty will last forever and ever, whereas here it can only fade."

For the first time the pretty lady was tempted, and the Devil knew it. He fetched a mirror from her bureau and held it up in front of her so she could look at herself. "Wouldn't it be a shame," he coaxed, "to let such a pretty face go to waste? If you stay here, it can only last fifteen or twenty more years, but in Hell there is no time. You will look just as you do now till the stars fall and a new plan is made, and we all know that will never happen."

The pretty lady looked at herself in the mirror and felt, as she sometimes did, that it *was* rather nice to be pretty, but in the nick of time she remembered what it was she really wanted. "Tell me," she said. "Is there any love in Hell?"

"Love?" said the Devil with a shudder. "What would we want with a thing like that?"

"Well then," said the pretty lady, pushing away the mirror, "I'll never agree to go. You can beg all you want from now till Sunday, but it won't be any use."

At this the Devil grew very angry and his eyes glowed like embers. "Is that your final word?" he demanded.

"That is my final word," she answered.

"Very well!" he said. "I can't take you against your will, that's true. But I can take your beauty. I can, and I will." There was another clap of thunder and the Devil disappeared in a cloud of smoke. He went straight back to Hell and took all the pretty lady's beauty with him, and he tacked it up in little fragments all over his throne room, where it sparkled and twinkled and brightened up the place very nicely.

After a couple of years, however, the Devil grew curious about the lady and went up to see how she was getting along. He arrived at her cottage at twilight and went to peer in through the window. And there she was, ugly as a boot, sitting down to supper. But candles lit the table and she was no longer alone. Sitting with her was a young man just as ugly as she, and in a cradle near her chair lay a very ugly baby. And the strange thing was that there was such love around the table that the Devil reeled back as if some-one had struck him.

"Humph!" said the Devil to himself. "I'll never understand this if I live to be a trillion!"

So he went back to Hell in a temper and tore down all the lady's beauty from the walls of his throne room and threw it away, and it floated up out of Hell into a dark corner of the sky and made itself, more usefully, into a new star.

THE HARPS OF
HEAVEN

THERE WERE two brothers in the World once
named Basil and Jack—Basil was the fat one—a pair
of mean, low, quarrelsome fellows who hated each
other right from the start and would never have stayed
together if it weren't for the fact that no one else
could stand them for a minute. They had begun to
fight when they were babies and fought all their lives,
so that one or the other was always black and blue;
but still they had gone into business together and had
managed to become quite famous, at least with the law,
for they were positively the best thieves in the World.

There wasn't anything that Basil and Jack couldn't

steal if they wanted to, and most of the time they wanted to. Then they would sell what they stole and spend all the money on whiskey and iodine, the first to get them ready for a fight and the second to patch them up afterward. But one night they went too far, for each in secret had bought a pistol, and in the middle of the fight they shot each other dead. However, this drastic event made very little difference between them, for when they arrived at the gates of Hell, which happened almost at once—there being no question in anyone's mind as to where they belonged—they began another fight on the spot over who should go in first.

When the Devil heard all the commotion, he was pleased as punch. "It's Basil and Jack!" he said to himself. "And not a moment too soon!"

Now, what the Devil meant by that was this: there was a peevish piano teacher in Hell—sent down for nagging—whose principal quarrel with the place was the music. There was bound to be better music in Heaven, she said, since they had so many lovely harps there, while in Hell, she said, there wasn't even one harp, lovely or otherwise.

The Devil had been stung by these remarks, for he was proud of Hell. But it was all too true that he had no harps, and he had decided that the only way to get a good one was to steal it from Heaven. And the only way to do *that* was to send up Basil and Jack. "If anyone can steal a harp from Heaven, it's Basil and Jack," he said to himself, "and now at last they're here!"

So, as soon as the brothers were settled in, the Devil had them brought to his throne room. "Basil and Jack!" he said joyfully. "Basil and Jack at last."

"That's us," said Jack.

And Basil said, "None other!"

"Splendid!" said the Devil. "I've got a job for you." And he went on to tell them the problem.

Well, the brothers were just as glad to get busy again, so they heard the Devil out, and the whole thing appealed to them hugely.

"That's the stuff," said Basil.

And Jack said, "Right!"

"You'll need a good plan, though," said the Devil. "A really good plan."

"Nothing to that," said the brothers. "There's no job anywhere too tricky for *us*."

"So I've heard," said the Devil, "and I hope it's true. I've set my heart, such as it is, on having a harp in Hell. I can't go up myself—they'd know me in a minute. But you two can do it if anyone can."

So Basil and Jack thought up a plan, and the plan was to disguise themselves as angels. "We'll just go up all sweet-like," they said, "and pretend to have lost our way. Then we'll slip in, grab the merchandise, slip out, and be back in time for supper."

"Splendid!" said the Devil, and he gave them the costumes they needed and sent them on their way.

It took a good while to get there, for they had to pass round the World on the way, and the wings the Devil gave them took time to get used to. But at least they didn't fight, for neither wanted to spoil his costume, and after a while they arrived at the gates of Heaven, out of breath but full of confidence.

Now, confidence is all right, but it isn't everything, for at this point things began to go wrong in ways that the brothers had never in the World expected. Here they were at the gates, but a Person was sitting there with a harp at his side, and this Person looked at them, looked at their costumes, smiled, and said at last in a gentle tone, "Why, it's Jack and Basil, isn't it? Let's see now. *You* must be Basil, because Basil is the fat one, and *you* must be Jack. What brings you up this way?"

"Oh," said Basil.

And Jack said, "Well . . ."

"Never mind," said the Person at the gates. "I already know why you've come. And I must say you look very nice in your costumes."

No one in all their lives had ever called the brothers nice, and Jack had it in mind to say, "Nuts!" But he didn't quite dare, somehow, and Basil just stood there with his mouth open.

"You're here for a harp," said the Person at the gates. "Well, that's all right. There are plenty of harps in Heaven, and this one here beside me is for you. There isn't any need to steal one."

"Oh!" said Jack.

And Basil said, "Well."

And they were both severely disappointed.

But the Person at the gates only smiled and picked up the harp—a small triangular harp made of gold, with cupids carved on its frame and strings like sunbeams—and handed it to them. "Goodbye then," said the Person at the gates.

So Jack took the harp and off the brothers went, back round the World to Hell.

It took a good deal longer to go down than it had to come up—a fact about which one may draw one's own conclusions—and the brothers, who were already cross about missing the chance to steal, soon grew bored with flying and began to argue.

"Here," said Basil. "Let *me* take the harp for a

while. There's no reason *you* should get to have it all the time."

"I'll be hanged if I will," said Jack. "You'd only drop it."

"Selfish!" said Basil.

And Jack said, "Clumsy!"

"Donkey!" said Basil.

"Pig!" said Jack.

"You're another."

"Am not."

"Are too."

And right there in the air between Heaven and Hell, Basil and Jack began to fight.

It was a glorious fight, with a great tearing of costumes, and a great snatching out of feathers from wings, and a great noise full of yells, thumps, swats, and wallops; and right in the middle was the poor little harp, yanked this way and that like tug of war.

They fought all the way back to Hell and arrived at last in terrible condition.

"Where's the harp?" said the Devil, who had heard them coming. "Hand it over." He took it away from them, cradled it in one arm, and ran his thumb across the strings.

But instead of sounding sweeter than zephyrs, the harp gave off a discord that made all three of them wince.

"*Now* see what you've done with your silly fighting," said the Devil. "My harp's all out of tune!"

"Oh," said Basil.

And Jack said, "Well."

"And I don't know how to tune it!" said the Devil.

"Neither do I," said Jack.

And Basil said, "Me either."

And that, of course, was that, for the pity of it was that there wasn't a soul—no one in all of Hell—who knew how to tune a harp from Heaven, not even the piano teacher.

"Well," said the Devil to Basil and Jack, "you'll just have to go back and get another."

"If you say so," said Basil and Jack.

"I do," said the Devil.

So back they went just as they were, in their ragged costumes, and the flying was harder than ever with so many feathers missing from their wings. But still they got there at last without too much complaining, and found the Person still sitting at the gates.

"Why, Jack and Basil! Here you are again!" said the Person.

"That's it," said Jack.

And Basil said, "Right."

But they were more than a little embarrassed.

"You've come for another harp, I expect," said the Person at the gates, observing the tears in their costumes.

"Right," said Basil.

And Jack said, "That's it."

"Nothing easier," said the Person. And he took another harp exactly like the first one from under his robe, and held it out to them.

This time Basil took the harp and off they started once again for Hell. But after they had been flying for a while, Jack couldn't stand it any longer. He gave Basil a poke and said, "I never saw anything so silly as you holding on to that harp."

"Says who?" said Basil.

"Says me," said Jack.

"Says pigs," said Basil.

And they were off again, fighting like a frenzy.

This time, however, in the middle of the fight, just when things were getting really satisfying, Basil dropped the harp. Down it fell, straight toward the World, and landed—clunk!—on a mountaintop.

"I told you so," said Jack.

Well, they flew down and found it and took it round the World to Hell just the same, and when they gave it to the Devil, he was very upset.

"Look at this harp!" he said. "It's all bashed out of shape! No one could play a harp in this condition."

"Someone can patch it up," said Basil.

"Ding it out with a hammer or something," said Jack.

But there wasn't a goldsmith in all of Hell who knew how to work on a harp from Heaven, and the piano teacher stood to one side and looked scornful.

"Back you go," said the Devil to the brothers. "One more time. And this time you'd better do it right."

"If you say so," said Basil and Jack.

"I do," said the Devil.

So back they had to go once more, and this time the Person at the gates sighed and shook his head when he saw them. "Jack and Basil!" he said. "Can it really be you again?"

"That's it," said Jack.

And Basil said, "Right."

But they were more embarrassed than ever.

"Well," said the Person at the gates, "there's one harp left. I hope you make it through with this one." And he handed them the third harp, went on into Heaven, and shut the gates behind him.

So Basil and Jack took the harp between them, with both holding on to it, and started back down again toward Hell. And this time they got all the way round the World before anything happened. In fact, they were almost to Hell when Basil's wings, which were in far worse shape than Jack's, came loose from his costume and there he was with no way to keep from falling except to cling to his half of the harp.

"Leave off!" cried Jack, flapping his own wings hard. "You'll drag us both down!"

"I can't leave off!" said Basil. "If I do, I'll fall."

"So fall!" said Jack. "Better you than both of us." And he tried to pry Basil's fingers loose from the harp.

They made quite a picture, there in the air above Hell, grappling and struggling, and in the midst of trying to get a safer grip, Basil snatched at the harp strings and pulled them right out like straws from a broom.

And that was the way they arrived back in Hell, Jack with the harp and Basil with the strings, and the

Devil was so angry that his horns smoked. "I'll go myself!" he bellowed. "And take my chances!"

"No use," said Basil.

"There's no harps left," said Jack.

"This was the last one," said both of them together.

And the pity of it was that there was no one in all of Hell who knew how to put the strings back into a harp from Heaven.

So the Devil had to give it up, angry or not. And to punish Jack and Basil, he made them take piano lessons from the peevish teacher—thereby punishing her as well, since the lessons went on for hundreds of years and the brothers never could learn anything but scales, no matter how much they practiced. And of course she made them practice all the time.

But the Devil kept the harps in his throne room just the same. "At least," he said to himself, "no one can say I don't *have* any." And he pretended to everyone that he could fix the harps any time he wanted to, but just didn't want to for now.

THE IMP
IN THE BASKET

T H E R E   W A S a clergyman once who was a very good and gentle man. He scrubbed the steps of the church every day and made his own candles for the altar, and he believed that everyone was just as good as he was himself. No matter how terrible the things were that people did, no matter how often they pounded each other and murdered each other and robbed and cheated and kicked their dogs, he would only sigh and say, "Ah, well, it was all a mistake, I'm sure. They didn't mean to do it." And he would say a prayer for them and was always sure they would mend their ways sooner or later.

One morning when the clergyman went out to scrub the steps of the church, he found a basket waiting and in the basket was a baby. "Aha!" said the clergyman. "Someone has left this baby here for me so I can raise it in the church in the ways of goodness!" And this pleased him very much. But when he picked up the basket and looked more closely, he saw that the baby was no ordinary baby. "Dear me!" he whispered. "Why, this baby is an imp! No doubt about it. A devil's baby with skin like a pepper, and the basket reeks of brimstone!" He set it down again at once, in horror, but the imp peered up at him so sweetly, smiling and smiling, that the clergyman was at a loss to know what to do. He left the basket where it was and went inside the church to sit down and have a talk with himself.

"A baby is a baby—helpless and in need of protection."

"Yes, but *this* baby can only grow up to be a demon!"

"And yet, suppose I could prevent that. Just suppose. Shouldn't I try?"

"Nonsense. It's been sent by the Devil to tempt me."

"Perhaps. But, on the other hand, it could have been sent by God to test me."

"That would be a test, to be sure, turning red into white."

"There now—it's starting to cry out there. It's hungry, no doubt, and tired after its journey."

"Its journey! What am I saying? Why, it must have come up straight from Hell."

"Nevertheless, a baby is a baby. I must do what I can."

And so, still unsure as to whether he was right or wrong, the clergyman carried the imp home to his cottage behind the churchyard.

Now, the clergyman saw at once that he would have to have food for the imp. "For," he thought, "a baby is a baby and mustn't be let to starve." So he hurried to a nearby farmhouse to buy a pail of milk.

"What!" said the farmer's wife. "A pail of milk? You've taken on a child at your age?"

"I have," said the clergyman nervously. "A baby. Left on the church steps."

He didn't say the baby was an imp. He was not at all sure what the farmer's wife might do when she learned about that. But his silence did him no good, for the farmer's wife turned business-like at once. "I'll come along and see to the little mite for you," she said. "What do *you* know about babies after all, an old bachelor like you?"

"No, no!" said the clergyman hastily. "I'll figure things out, no doubt. Don't trouble yourself."

"Twaddle," said the farmer's wife. "It's no trouble."

And he couldn't put her off.

When they came to the clergyman's cottage, the farmer's wife stopped suddenly and sniffed. "Brimstone!" she said. "Smoke and brimstone! Quick, save the baby—your cottage must be on fire!"

But it wasn't. When they went inside, the smell of brimstone was very strong, but everything was peaceful. The imp had gone to sleep in its basket. The farmer's wife went right away to look at it, and when she saw what it was, her mouth fell open. "Why, it's a devil's baby!" she gasped. "An imp!" And she turned and ran out of the cottage. "A devil!" she yelled as she ran. "A devil at the very doors of the church! Help! Help! We'll all of us be cursed!"

"No, wait!" cried the clergyman, wringing his hands in the doorway. "Stop! It's only a baby, and a baby is a baby, isn't it?" And he was quite overcome with doubt.

But the farmer's wife went running all around the village, raising a great crowd of people, and in no time at all they were gathered round the clergyman's cottage. "Come out!" they demanded. "Come out at once and leave the imp behind. We'll burn the cottage down and the imp with it. It's the only way to get rid of it."

When he heard this, the clergyman was horrified and his doubt dissolved. "You can't do that!" he answered firmly. "A baby is a baby, imp or not. Helpless, and in need of protection. And anyway, perhaps the imp can be raised in the ways of goodness. The Devil was an angel once, wasn't he? So there must be hope, even for an imp!"

But the people said to each other, "He's mad! He's out of his senses!" And they called to him again: "Come out and let us burn the cottage down!"

"Never," said the clergyman. "I can't abandon a baby, imp or not. If you burn down the cottage, you must burn it down with both of us inside."

The people conferred among themselves and decided it was too late to save the clergyman anyway; the Devil had most certainly possessed him. There was only one thing to do. They brought a torch and set fire to the cottage with the clergyman and the imp, both of them, inside.

The clergyman stood holding the basket as the flames shot up around him, and prayed a long prayer, for he was very much afraid. But the imp woke up and when it saw the smoke and fire it clapped its little hands and crowed with delight.

Outside, the people stood back from the heat and watched the cottage burn, and now it was their turn to doubt. "Of course it *was* only a baby after all, and suppose it *could* have been raised in the ways of goodness," they said to each other. "Just suppose."

However, it was far too late to put out the fire, for the cottage was small and dry. The roof began to buckle and then it fell in, and the walls fell in around it. But when the smoke cleared, there stood the clergyman in the middle of the mess with his eyes tight shut, entirely unharmed, and the imp and the basket were gone.

The people were amazed, and then they were thankful, and then they were jubilant. "A miracle!" they cried. "Our clergyman has been saved by God from death!" And as a gesture of their relief and gratitude, they went to work at once to build a new cottage so the clergyman could have his own place once again.

The clergyman took up his life and duties without a murmur, but for a time he was greatly troubled. Had he really been saved by God, as the people supposed, or had he perhaps—just perhaps—been saved by the Devil? However, he never spoke of this question to anyone. He continued to make candles for the altar, and every morning he came out to scrub the steps of the church. He had noticed at once, of course, the sooty spot on the top step where the imp's basket had rested, and he tried very hard to scrub it away. But no matter how hard he scrubbed, the spot remained as clear as ever. So at last he brought from inside the church a pot of sickly ivy and set it there. The ivy flourished, standing on the spot, which was strange; but the clergyman scrubbed around it every morning and was glad of it anyway, and to the end of his days he never saw another imp.

NUTS

ONE DAY the Devil was sitting in his throne room eating walnuts from a large bag and complaining, as usual, about the terrible nuisance of having to crack the shells, when all at once he had an idea. "The best way to eat walnuts," he said to himself, "is to trick someone else into cracking them for you."

So he fetched a pearl from his treasure room, opened the next nut very carefully with a sharp knife so as not to spoil the shell, and put the pearl inside along with the meat. Then he glued the shell back together. "Now all I have to do," he said, "is give this walnut to some greedy soul who'll find the pearl in it and insist on opening the lot to look for more!"

So he dressed himself as an old man with a long beard and went up into the World, taking along his nutcracker and the bag of walnuts with the special nut right on top. And he sat himself down by a country road to wait.

Pretty soon a farm wife came marching along.

"Hey, there!" said the Devil. "Want a walnut?"

The farm wife looked at him shrewdly and was at once suspicious, but she didn't let on for a minute. "All right," she said. "Why not?"

"That's the way," said the Devil, chuckling to himself. And he reached into the bag and took out the special walnut and gave it to her.

However, much to his surprise, she merely cracked the nut open, picked out the meat and ate it, and threw away the shell without a single word or comment. And then she went on her way and disappeared.

"That's strange," said the Devil with a frown. "Either she swallowed my pearl or I gave her the wrong walnut to begin with."

He took out three more nuts that were lying on top
of the pile, cracked them open, and ate the meat, but
there was no pearl to be seen. He opened and ate four
more. Still no pearl. And so it went, on and on all after-
noon, till the Devil had opened every walnut in the
bag, all by himself after all, and had made a terrible
mess on the road with the shells. But he never did find
the pearl, and in the end he said to himself, "Well,
that's that. She swallowed it." And there was nothing
for it but to go back down to Hell. But he took along
a stomach ache from eating all those nuts, and a temper
that lasted for a week.

In the meantime the farm wife went on to market,
where she took the pearl out from under her tongue,
where she'd been saving it, and she traded it for two
turnips and a butter churn and went on home again
well pleased.

We are not all of us greedy.

A

PALINDROME

THERE WAS an artist once who was so kind and good and loving that everyone who knew him liked to say he was "the best fellow in the World." But the pictures he painted struck a lot of people as being most remarkably evil, for they all showed blank-faced men and women hopping about with their clothes off, or chopping each other into little pieces, and in general behaving in ways unacceptable to decent society.

In spite of this, the people who knew him, loving him as they did, were more than willing to accept and admire the artist's pictures. He was very skillful after all, quite a master, and some of his friends, believing there is good and evil in everyone, liked to think that all the evil in the artist came out in his work and left behind nothing but good in the man himself.

Now, the Devil knew about the artist's pictures and thought they were magnificent. Sometimes, in fact, he would come up out of Hell in the middle of the night for the sole purpose of hanging about in the studio, admiring them. "Wouldn't it be splendid," he would think to himself, "if we had such a fellow for Number One Artist at home!" And then he would go away shaking his head, for he knew, as well as he knew anything, that the artist was too good a man to end up at an easel in Hell.

The Devil pondered this problem off and on for a long time and after a few years he had an idea. The artist had completed thirty-seven pictures. "When he makes it to forty," said the Devil to himself, "I'll just go up there and steal them all and hang them down here in my gallery. Forty is enough, anyway. And then I'll steal all his canvas, paints, and brushes, and even his easel—after which we'll just sit back and see what happens."

The artist didn't know of the Devil's plan, of course. He went on calmly with his work, creating pictures of unmatchable evil, and whenever he went out, little children would follow him and birds would perch on his shoulders, and people would say: "Here comes the artist! What a good fellow he is, in spite of his terrible pictures—surely the best fellow in the World!"

It wasn't long, however, before the fortieth picture was completed, and when that time came, the Devil, true to his plan, sneaked up out of Hell and stole the whole kit and caboodle. He dropped the easel, brushes, and things in a dusty corner of his throne room, but he hung the pictures in his gallery and they were a huge success, with streams of the damned and all manner of major and minor demons filing through every day to study them approvingly over a cup of punch.

Up in the World the artist, meanwhile, was baffled

by what had happened. He asked around his village, but no one knew anything at all about the disappearance of the pictures, and even less about the theft of the easel and the rest. The artist grew very worried because he was a poor man who earned the money for his tools by digging holes, since no one ever bought his pictures, and he knew that he would have to dig holes for a very long time before he had enough money to begin again.

"Lovely!" said the Devil when word came to him in Hell of the artist's distress. "Now we shall see what we shall see." And he sat back and smiled and waited.

As day after day went by, with no more pictures to work on and nothing to do but dig, the artist began to alter. He stopped smiling, and chased little children away when they tried to follow him, and shooed the birds from his shoulders. He grew silent and ill-tempered and even cast off from the friends who loved him. And when he walked scowling in the village, the people would move out of his way and say to each

other: "Here comes the artist. What a terrible fellow he is after all, just like the pictures he used to paint!"

The Devil was enormously pleased by these developments. His plan was working perfectly. "I'll have the fellow himself in the end, as well as his pictures," he said, and he sat back and smiled and waited some more.

One day, however, as the artist was digging holes in the earth, he came to a rich layer of clay. He scooped out a large lump and put it aside, and when the day was over he took it home to his studio. All night he worked with it and when morning came he had finished a little statue. Strange to say, however, the statue showed a mother bending over to touch a small child clinging to her skirts, and the mood of it was one of great goodness and love.

This was the beginning of a new life for the artist. He modeled more and more small statues, similar to the first, and people liked them so much that he sold every one and didn't need to dig any more except when he needed more clay. Soon he could afford to work in stone, and as his fame spread, he was asked to carve fine marble statues and these in time could be found in every great church and courtyard in the land.

But the artist's ill temper grew worse and worse as his statues grew more and more loving. He became at last quite the opposite of what he had been before. And the people who had once been his friends, still believing there is good and evil in everyone, said it seemed as if all the good in the artist came out in his work and left behind nothing but evil in the man himself.

The Devil was hard put to understand what had gone wrong. On the one hand he was well pleased with the kind of man the artist had become, but at the same time he was disgusted with the statues. "That fellow is as useless to me now as he was before, and I don't know what to do," he said with a gnash of teeth. "So I will do the best thing: just forget all about him."

And that's what the Devil did. He forgot about the artist altogether and turned his attention to other things. As for the artist, nobody knows what became of him.

His paintings are admired in Hell to this day, and his statues are admired in Heaven, but the man himself seems to have been lost somewhere in between. No matter. He's sure to have plenty of company.

ASHES

THERE WAS a very bad man once, a certain Mr. Bezzle, who made a great deal of money by cheating shamefully, and on his death, which happened all of a sudden and was the plain result of too much roasted pig, his wife had his body cremated and kept the ashes in a silver urn on the mantelpiece, where it was nice and warm. This was entirely appropriate, though she may not have known it, for her husband had gone directly to Hell when he died, and was every bit as nice and warm there as his ashes were up in the World.

Now, it happened that Mrs. Bezzle, grown lonesome with her husband gone, took on a large, ill-mannered dog to keep her company. "He's got whiskers and he snores," she told her friends, "so it's just like having Bezzle back again." She was devoted to the dog and spoiled him dreadfully, even to the point of allowing him to gnaw bones in the house, though this practice was a great annoyance to the housemaid, whose task it was to keep things tidy.

One day, on coming across a greasy pork bone on the hearthrug, the housemaid, in a fit of temper, seized it and flung it into the fire, where it burned away to ashes with no one any the wiser. And then, on the next day, when the housemaid was at her daily chores, the handle of her broom bumped Mr. Bezzle's urn and down it fell onto the hearth, spilling that bad man's earthly remains into the fireplace.

"Horrors!" said the housemaid, and then she looked around. Mrs. Bezzle was nowhere in sight. "Oh, well," said the housemaid, and she knelt down and carefully scooped the ashes back into the urn with the fire shovel.

This was all very well, perhaps, and one way out of a bad situation, but the trouble was that some of Mr.

Bezzle's ashes had got mixed with the ashes in the fireplace; and some of the ashes in the fireplace were the ashes of the pork bone which the housemaid had thrown into the fire the day before. So what happened was that the pork-bone ashes got into the urn too, where they clearly didn't belong, and no one knew a thing about it.

Next morning, down in Hell, the Devil was sitting in his throne room writing poems when Mr. Bezzle came in and demanded an interview.

"What's the problem?" asked the Devil, going on with his writing.

"Problem?" cried Bezzle. *"Problem?* Why, look for yourself!"

So the Devil looked and saw that a large pig had come in with Mr. Bezzle and was standing pressed against his legs, looking up at him fondly.

"What are you doing with that pig?" asked the Devil.

"What am *I* doing?" cried Bezzle. "What is *it* doing? That's the question. See here now. Everything's gone along well since I came down. Good company, plenty to eat and drink, a nice room all to myself. Then yesterday this pig appears out of nowhere, follows me about like a puppy, and even insists on getting into bed with me. I don't know where it came from, and I don't know why or how. Do you?"

"I haven't the least idea," said the Devil.

"Well, something has to be done," said Bezzle, trying to push the pig away, though this seemed to be entirely useless, seeing as the pig merely pressed the closer and continued to gaze up at Bezzle with a look of great warmth and affection in its little red eyes.

"It's a nice enough pig," observed the Devil, peering at it, "and quite attached to you, evidently."

"Never mind that," said Bezzle. "Just do something. I really don't want to spend Eternity stomach to stomach with a pig."

"I'll ask around," said the Devil. "No doubt we can figure things out."

So Bezzle went away, the pig at his heels, and the Devil called in a couple of scholars, who looked through a couple of books; and the next day, when Bezzle came back, the Devil said, "It appears that you must have been buried with the pig, somehow or other."

"Impossible," said Bezzle. "I was cremated. And my wife keeps my ashes in an urn on the mantelpiece."

"Oh?" said the Devil. "Well, still, you're mixed up with the pig somewhere along the line. It's the only explanation."

"Then I'll just have to get unmixed," said Bezzle, moving his feet so the pig—who of course was still with him—wouldn't step on his toes. "One more night like the last two and I'll be crackers."

So the Devil went up to the World to Bezzle's house and when no one was looking he stole the urn, brought it down to Hell, and dumped out its contents in a quiet corner. "Well, there they are," he said to Bezzle. "You'll have to pick out the pig's part yourself, assuming you can tell the difference."

"There's got to be a difference between my ashes and a pig's," said Bezzle. And he set to work at once with high hopes, tweezers, and a large magnifying glass.

Day after day Bezzle sat in the corner, working away, while the pig rested its chin on his knee and gazed at him, and after a year he had separated a thimbleful of ashes that he thought must be the pig's because they were a slightly different shade of gray. After two years, and two thimblesful, it appeared that he was right, for the pig seemed less attentive. Its gaze was sometimes distracted from Bezzle's face, and it took to spending an hour or two, now and then, wandering off by itself. Bezzle was delighted, and attacked his work with fresh vigor.

And then, after three years, when the task was nearly done and the pig was only coming by for lunch, Mrs. Bezzle's housemaid died of ill temper and arrived in Hell, still clutching her broom. And the first thing she noticed was the two piles of ashes, left alone for

a moment in the quiet corner where Bezzle had been laboring so long.

"This place is a mess," said the housemaid.

And she swept the two piles into one pile, swept the one pile into her dustpan, carried it all out, and buried it by the gates.

All Bezzle ever knew was that one minute the ashes were gone and the next minute the pig was back full time. Still, after a while, when the first rude shock had worn away, he grew resigned to having the pig around. They were together day and night, after all, and there was nothing for it but to make do. But Bezzle, in time, did more than that. He found that the pig was really rather good company and altogether his best friend in the place. Before a hundred years were out, he had even managed to teach it to play gin rummy, though it cheated shamefully. As for the house-maid, she settled down in another part of Hell and kept her fireplace—and her hearthrug—shining clean.

PERFECTION

THERE WAS a little girl once called Angela who always did everything right. In fact, she was perfect. She had better manners than anyone, and not only that, but she hung up her clothes and never forgot to feed the chickens. And not only *that,* but her hair was always combed and she never bit her fingernails. A lot of people, all of them fair-to-middling, disliked her very much because of this, but Angela didn't care. She just went right on being perfect and let things go as they would.

Now, when the Devil heard about Angela, he was revolted. "Not," he explained to himself, "that I give a hang about children as a rule, but *this* one! Imagine what she'll be like when she grows up—a woman whose only fault is that she has no faults!" And the very thought of it made him cross as crabs. So he wrote up a list of things to do that he hoped would make Angela edgy and, if all went well, even make her lose her temper. "Once she loses her temper a few times," said the Devil, "she'll never be perfect again."

However, this proved harder to do than the Devil had expected. He sent her chicken pox, then poison ivy, and then a lot of mosquito bites, but she never scratched and didn't even seem to itch. He arranged for a cow to step on her favorite doll, but she never shed a tear. Instead, she forgave the cow at once, in public, and said it didn't matter. Next the Devil fixed it so that for weeks on end her cocoa was always too hot and her oatmeal too cold, but this, too, failed to make her angry. In fact, it seemed that the worse things were, the better Angela liked it, since it gave her a chance to show just how perfect she was.

Years went by. The Devil used up every idea on his list but one, and Angela still had her temper, and her manners were still better than anyone's. "Well, anyway," said the Devil to himself, "my last idea can't miss. That much is certain." And he waited patiently for the proper moment.

When that moment came, the Devil's last idea worked like anything. In fact, it was perfect. As soon as he made it happen, Angela lost her temper once a day at least, and sometimes oftener, and after a while she had lost it so often that she was never quite so perfect again.

And how did he do it? Simple. He merely saw that she got a perfect husband and a perfect house, and then—he sent her a fair-to-middling child.

THE ROSE AND
THE MINOR DEMON

THERE WAS a minor demon once, a wistful, senti-mental creature who really didn't belong in Hell at all, though Heaven knows there was nowhere else for him to go. And the Devil was embarrassed to have him around because he was so different from everyone else. So a job was found for him which kept him out of sight, and this job was to guard the Devil's treasure room.

The minor demon worked at his task every day, which is to say that he sat in the treasure room with nothing to do, since no one ever came near the place; and while he sat there, he would fall to mooning over all the thousand objects that filled the shelves, everything from silver pitchers to golden calves. But the object he mooned over most was a large porcelain vase which had a lot of roses painted on it. The roses, he thought, were lovely, all colors of the rainbow, and he wished like anything that there were roses just like them in Hell.

But there were no roses of any kind in Hell, or rainbows either, for that matter. And yet, the more he mooned about it, the more the minor demon wanted some, and at last he went to the Devil to ask if he could have a garden.

"Well now," said the Devil. "That's a funny thing to ask for. What in the World do you want a garden for?"

"I just want to plant things," said the minor demon. "Flowers."

"Flowers?" exclaimed the Devil. "What kind of flowers?"

"Oh," said the minor demon nervously, "just some roses or something."

"Ugh!" said the Devil. "Roses? In Hell? Where did you get an idea like that?"

"From the porcelain vase in the treasure room," said the minor demon, and then he blushed a darker shade of red than he was already. "I guess," he confessed, "I've got a soft spot in my heart for roses."

"What kind of a minor demon are you anyway?" said the Devil in exasperation. "A soft spot? In your heart? You haven't got a heart. And as for soft spots, you know what they say about that. A soft spot in an apple means it's going bad, and one bad apple can spoil a barrelful. So let's have no more talk about soft spots and hearts. Or roses, either. Roses are entirely out of the question. If you really want a garden, you can have one, I suppose, but you'll have to plant sensible things. Like henbane or hemlock or aconite."

"All right," said the minor demon sadly, and he went away to a quiet place and hoed up the ground and planted henbane and hemlock and aconite and even a little deadly nightshade. But he wasn't satisfied, not even when all the things he had planted grew like weeds, which is after all exactly what they were. For he still wanted roses.

At last he could stand it no longer. He crept out of Hell one night, which was quite against the rules for minor demons, and made his way up to the World, where everything was sweet with May; and he stole a little rosebush and brought it back down and planted it at the back of his garden, with the hemlock growing up tall around it to hide it from view.

The minor demon was amazed at his own daring and trembled very much to think what might happen when the deed was discovered. But for a long while no one suspected that the rosebush was there. Even the Devil, passing by, admired the hemlock and the deadly nightshade, and told the minor demon that the garden was a good idea. But then one morning one of the buds on the rosebush opened into a blossom, white and silky as a baby's fist.

The minor demon was enchanted when he saw the

blossom, but right away he was frightened too. For although it was just like the roses on the porcelain vase, and most enormously pleasing, it had one thing the painted roses didn't have, and that one thing was fragrance. The minor demon hadn't known about the fragrance. And now the air all over that part of Hell was rich with it.

Up rose the Devil in his throne room, sniffing like Jack in the Beanstalk's giant, except that he didn't say "Fee fie foe fum." Instead, he said, "What's that smell?" and wrinkled up his nose. And he trailed around, up and down, looking for it everywhere.

But the minor demon, afraid that exactly this would happen, had hurriedly picked the single blossom and buried it, so that the fragrance drifted off at last and disappeared.

"Humph!" said the Devil. "Must have been a bad dream." And he put it out of his mind and went back to his usual business.

The minor demon grieved for the buried flower.

"But what else could I have done?" he reflected with a sigh. And next morning, of course, the same thing happened again. Another blossom opened, spilled its fragrance, and had to be picked and buried.

This time, however, the Devil knew that the smell he smelled was not a dream after all. "It's that pesty minor demon, that's what it is," he said to himself. "He's got a rosebush in that garden of his or I miss my guess. And tomorrow I'll catch him red-handed."

So the morning after, the Devil got up early and went directly to the minor demon's garden, where he found that the smell of roses was powerful indeed. And of course it took no time at all to uncover the rosebush, back behind the hemlock, with another heavy blossom nodding on its stem. Not only that, but there crouched the minor demon in the very act of picking it.

"Aha!" cried the Devil triumphantly. "What have we here?"

The minor demon was a wistful, sentimental creature, to be sure, but still he could be quick when he had to

be. So, although he trembled, he thought for an instant and said, "It's harvest time. I'm harvesting my thorns."

"Thorns, my grandmother," said the Devil. "That's a rosebush."

"Oh no, sir," said the minor demon. "Excuse me, but this is a *thorn* bush. Why, just see for yourself. It's got many more thorns than blossoms. I planted it especially, and I'm giving all the thorns to you when the crop is in."

"Indeed!" said the Devil. "Well, the fact is, that white thing you're holding there happens to be a rose."

"Dear me!" said the minor demon. "Is it really? Isn't that a shame! And the thorns were so ideal."

The Devil knew perfectly well that the minor demon knew the bush was a rosebush. And what's more, the minor demon knew the Devil knew he knew it. But still, the idea of a crop of thorns was appealing to the Devil, for thorns were useful in a number of ways. So at last he merely shrugged and said, "Very well. You can be my first and only thorn farmer if you want to.

But pull up that terrible rosebush at once and plant a nice big cactus instead. Oh, and while you're at it, take a can of black enamel and give that porcelain vase a good thick coat. There'll be no roses of any kind in Hell as long as I'm around."

So the minor demon had to pull up the rosebush and throw it away and plant a cactus behind the hemlock, and this made him very sad. And it made him even sadder to paint the porcelain vase. Still, he knew he was lucky to get off with so small a punishment, so he tended his garden without another murmur and harvested many a bumper crop of thorns.

He kept on guarding the treasure room as well, though it gave him no pleasure to look at the porcelain vase now that it was painted black. And then one day long after, the Devil came in for some reason or other, and when he saw the vase, he said, "What's that ugly thing doing in here? Take it out and throw it away." For he had forgotten all about the roses.

Well, the minor demon did as the Devil asked. He

took the porcelain vase out and dropped it on the trash pile. But when it landed, it broke into a great many pieces and some of the black enamel chipped off. And there, on one of the fragments where the paint had come away, a rose was clearly visible, looking white and silky as a baby's fist.

Then the minor demon took the fragment and filed down its sharp and jagged edges, and carried it home to keep under his pillow forever and ever. And in this way he had a treasure of his own, which made Hell a little nicer place for him to be even if he didn't belong there, since Heaven knows there was nowhere else for him to go. The painted rose wasn't as good as the real thing, of course, but still it was better than nothing. And knowing it was there under his pillow made the minor demon happy in a small and secret way that no one ever knew about but him.

THE POWER OF
SPEECH

A LOT of people believe that once a day every goat in the World has to go down to Hell to have his beard combed by the Devil, but this is obvious nonsense. The Devil doesn't have time to comb the beards of all the goats in the World even if he wanted to, which of course he doesn't. Who would? There are far too many goats in the first place, and in the second place their beards are nearly all in terrible condition, full of snarls, burrs, and dandelion juice.

Nevertheless, whether he wants to comb their beards or not, the Devil is as fond of goats as he is of anything, and always has one or another somewhere about, kept on as a sort of pet. He treats them pretty well too, considering, and the goats give back as good or as bad as they get, which is one reason why the Devil likes them so much, for goats are one hundred percent unsentimental.

Now, there was a goat in the World once that the Devil had had his eye on for some time, a great big goat with curving horns and a prize from every fair for miles around. "I want that goat," said the Devil to himself, "and I mean to have him even if he has to be dragged down here by his beard." But that was a needless thing to say, and the Devil knew it, for animals, and especially goats, are nothing at all like people when it comes to right and wrong. Animals don't see much to choose between the two. So, Heaven or Hell, it's all one to them, especially goats. All the Devil had to do was go up there, to the cottage that the goat called home, and lead him away.

The only trouble was that the old woman who owned the goat was no dummy. She knew how much the Devil liked goats and she also knew how much he hated bells. So she kept the goat—whose name was Walpurgis—tied up to a tree in her yard and she fastened a little bell around his neck with a length of ribbon. Walpurgis hated bells almost as much as the Devil did; but there was no way he could say so and nothing he could do about his own bell except to stand very still in order to keep it from jangling. This led some passers-by to conclude that he was only a stuffed goat put there for show and not a real goat at all. So many people came up to the old woman's door to ask about it that at last she put up a sign which said: THIS IS A REAL GOAT. And after that she got a little peace and quiet. Not that any of it mattered to Walpurgis, who didn't give a hoot for what anybody thought one way or another.

The Devil didn't care what anybody thought either. But he still wanted the goat. He turned the whole problem of the bell over in his mind, considering this solution and that, and at last, hoping something would occur to him, he went up out of Hell to the old woman's door to have a little talk with her. "See here," he said as soon as she answered his knock. "I mean to have your goat."

The old woman looked him up and down, and wasn't in the least dismayed. "Go ahead and take him," she said. "If you can do that, he's yours."

The Devil glanced across the yard to where Walpurgis stood tied up to the tree. "If I try to untie him, that bell will ring, and I can't stand bells," he said with a shudder.

"I know," said the old woman, looking satisfied.

The Devil swallowed his annoyance and tried a more familiar tack. "I'll give you anything you want," he said, "if you'll go over there and take away that wretched bell. I'll even make you Queen of the World."

The old woman cackled. "I've got my cottage, my goat, and everything I need," she said. "Why should I want to buy trouble? There's nothing you can do for me."

The Devil ground his teeth. "It takes a mean mind

to put a bell on a goat," he snapped. "If he were *my* goat, I'd never do that. I'll bet a bucket of brimstone he hates that bell."

"Save your brimstone," said the old woman. "He's only a goat. It doesn't matter to *him*."

"He'd tell you, though, if he could talk," said the Devil.

"May be," said the old woman. "I've often wished he *could* talk, if it comes to that. But until he can, I'll keep him any way I want to. So goodbye." And she slammed the door between them.

This gave the Devil the very idea he was looking for. He hurried down to Hell and was back in a minute with a little cake into which he had mixed the power of speech, and he tossed it to Walpurgis. The goat chewed it up at once and swallowed it and then the Devil changed himself into a field mouse and hid in the grass to see what would happen.

After a while Walpurgis shook himself, which made the bell jangle, and at that he opened his mouth and said a very bad word. An expression of great surprise came over his face when he heard himself speak, and his eyes opened wide. Then they narrowed again and he tried a few more bad words, all of which came out clear and unmistakable. Then, as much as goats can ever smile, Walpurgis smiled. He moved as far from the tree as the rope would allow, and called out in a rude voice: "Hey there, you in the cottage!"

The old woman came to the door and put her head out. "Who's there?" she asked suspiciously, peering about.

"It's me! Walpurgis!" said the goat. "Come out here and take away this bell."

"You *can* talk, then!" observed the old woman.

"I can," said Walpurgis. "And I want this bell off. Now. And be quick about it."

The old woman stared at the goat and then she folded her arms. "I had no idea you'd be this kind of goat," she said.

"To the Devil with that," said Walpurgis carelessly.

"What's the difference? It's this bell I'm talking about. Come over here and take it off."

"I can't," said the old woman. "If I do, the Devil will steal you away for sure."

"If you don't," said the goat, "I'll yell and raise a ruckus."

"Yell away," said the old woman. "I've got no choice in the matter that I can see." And she went back inside the cottage and shut the door.

So Walpurgis began to yell. He yelled all the bad words he knew and he yelled them loud and clear, and he yelled them over and over till the countryside rang with them, and before long the old woman came out of her cottage with her fingers in her ears. "Stop that!" she shouted at the goat.

Walpurgis stopped yelling. "Do something, then," he said.

"All right, I will!" said the old woman. "And serve you both right. If I'd known what kind of a goat you were, I'd have done it in the first place. The Devil deserves a goat like you." She took away the bell and set Walpurgis free and right away the Devil leaped up from the grass and took the goat straight back to Hell.

Now the funny thing about the power of speech is that the Devil could give it away but he couldn't take it back. For a while it was amusing to have a talking goat in Hell, but not for very long, because Walpurgis complained a lot. He'd always been dissatisfied but being able to say so made all the difference. The air was too hot, he said, or the food was too dry, or there was just plain nothing to do but stand around. "I might as well be wearing a bell again, for all the moving about I do in this place," said Walpurgis.

"Don't mention bells!" said the Devil.

This gave Walpurgis the very idea he was looking for. He began to yell all the bell-ringing words he knew. He yelled them loud and clear—clang, ding, jingle, bong—and he yelled them over and over till Hell rang with them.

At last the Devil rose up with his fingers in his ears. "Stop that!" he shouted at the goat.

Walpurgis stopped yelling. "Do something, then," he said.

"All right, I will!" said the Devil. And with that he changed Walpurgis into a stuffed goat and took him back up to the old woman's cottage and left him there in the yard, tied up to the tree.

When the old woman saw that the goat was back, she hurried out to see how he was. And when she *saw* how he was, she said to herself, "Well, that's what comes of talking too much." But she put the bell around his neck and kept him standing there anyway, and since the sign was still there too, and still said THIS IS A REAL GOAT, nobody ever knew the difference. And everyone, except Walpurgis, was satisfied.

DATE DUE

DATE DUE			
MAY 15	SEP 18		
OCT 27			
NOV 11			
NOV 16			
MAR 23			
MAR 30			
SEP 9			
JAN 10			
FEB 21			
APR 18			
NOV			